The Bard of the Blanco
Poems of Ernie Lee

Other works by Ernie Lee

Professional Texts and Workbooks

Contracting for Control and Disposal of Hazardous Materials, 1993, Southwest Logistics Institute (out of print)

Public Procurement Professions, 6 vol. Published by: University of Texas, Extended Learning program, 1997, 1998 (reprint) (out of print)

Risk Management for Buyers e-Group & Associates, Extended Learning program, Training Module, 2012 (reprint) (out of print)

Analysis Techniques for Buyers, e-Group & Associates, Extended Learning program, Training Module, 2013 (reprint) (out of print)

Economics for Buyers, e-Group & Associates, Extended Learning program, Training Module, 2013 (reprint) (out of print)

The Ring of Gyges, Ethics When No One is Watching, e-Group & Associates, Extended Learning program, Training Module, 2013 (reprint) (out of print)

The Bard of the Blanco

by

Ernie Lee

Aim-Hi Publishing

First Edition: [February 2017]
Printed in the United States of America
Aim-Hi Publishing LLC
1542 Lakeside Dr. West
Canyon Lake, Texas 78133
www.ernieleepoetry.com
Publisher's Catalog in-publication Data
Names: Lee, Ernest (Ernie), 1946- ;
Title: Where the Wild Rice Grows / by: Ernie Lee
Description: Aim-Hi Publishing, LLC, | 2017 Summary: A collection of poems by Ernie Lee
Library of Congress Control Number: **2017901259**

ISBN: 978-0-9971284-3-7 (Mass Market Paperback)

Subjects: Poetry | Texas | Tonkawa | Hill Country | humor | philosophy

9 8 7 6 5 4 3 2 1

WRITING IS GIVING

The author is pleased to announce that 2,016 copies of this book will be provided free of charge to **Teachers** because they know how to **Share.**
If you, or someone you know is a teacher and would like to have a free copy of this book, please a) go to www.ernieleepoetry.com, b) sign up on the website, and (c) nominate your recipient. Please give recipient's name, e-mail address, and preferred electronic format (i.e. .pdf, e-Pub, or Kindle, etc.) A book will be donated in your name as a free gift.

This campaign is made possible by the sale of books purchased on Amazon, Barnes & Noble, and other retail book outlets. No purchase is necessary, but is dearly appreciated.

Table of Contents

Life is Funny that Way

Love and Other Illusions

The Bard of the Blanco

Blanco River Valley

Bubbles forth from beneath the ground, cold and clear and perfect,
Water pools 'neath live oak trees
In sunny summer shade.
Source

Separate pools accumulate amongst the trees and ridged rocks
Bleed their liquid produce forth
Into shallow silted basins.
Blanco

Beneath shaded cliffs and limestone marls, past mossy marble boulders
Moisture strains through stone of honeycomb
Beneath the ancient Cypress.
Golden

Southeasterly now it runs, past moon-pale cliffs, sentinels of stone,
Swings and dips unseen below; bubbles forth to rise again.
Fuller. Faster. Fresher.
Frio.

Other springs now join the flow beneath the blue, deep Texas sky.
Playful splashes on shallow riffs the hot sun evaporates.
The gain outweighs the loss.

Moving.

Turkeys roost on grassy knolls, color-strewn 'neath
blankets bright,
While hillocks echo garbled, gobbled calls of love
As deer browse verdant valleys.
Serene.

Stair-step hills, like balconies; escarpment crippled
Dolomite,
Appear where hidden leaks and seeps carve caverns deep
In soft chalk limestone marl.
Karst.

Dropping now beneath the hills, wider, slower, richer
still,
And deeper yet, the chroma-blend of sky on water
mirrors
The blue-green hue of peaceful far-off places.
Shady.

Wild bees leave their honey trees; Quiet places – cool
oasis
Sweetness free for the taking
Sustains the hungry soul.
Paradise.

Wends and bends now past Pecan, joins in wedlock
fuller streams.
Home for man for untold time –
San Marcos – below the springs.

Haven.   Heaven.   Blanco.

Devil's Backbone

Deep in the shadowed canyons of the Devil's
Backbone heights
The haunted hills reverberate with a thousand years
of pain
Where Comanche ruled these steep stepped halls.
Beneath the
          vast, starry nights,
Coyote calls echoed from walls, when the moon
would rise again.

The full-faced moon shows the pearly rock a
creamy shade of
          light.
The turkey gobbles for a mate, and bats swoop and
swirl around.
The antlered bucks in velvet prongs rear up to train
for fight.
And the wind sings songs the whole night long;
exulting in the
          sound.

Sit with me on a morning ledge and watch the
storms roll by.
The dry earth seems to yearn to touch the healing
bliss of rain.
With forked tongue, lightning leaps to cliffs from
darkened sky.
The rain rolls down to hueco seeps, and the desert
blooms again.

Lie in the crystal sparkling stream, with water up to your ears.
Hear the rippled history of the stone and ancient men.
The song of Blanco River passed down through the ageless years.
You lie in the river and shiver and frown when the air is a hundred
            and ten.

The Whippoorwills in crevassed hills sing songs of countless woes
That deny the beauty of the place, and makes the stone a liar.
The fireflies glow on the old Blanco down where the wild rice
            grows
And the fifteen feet the sotol grows, and the agave even higher.

Despite the fractured plain, the toil and pain, and the evil name,
You can stand upon a lofty ledge, and feel the winds of history.
There is a beauty in the place that brings you back again
To feel the breath upon your face, and marvel in the mystery.

First appeared in The Hill Country Sun, <u>Bard of the Blanco</u>
August 2014

Clouds

Like great, voluminous, ocean-going tall ships,
slowly moving across the royal, blue deep,
clouds respond in unison to the varied winds,
rising white, billowed sheets against the sky.
Heavy laden, they seek some unknown port
where they are bound to discharge
their holds in raucous fervor.

Slowly, methodically, unstoppable,
They pass like the days of our lives.
Each different, and each bound on a sure course -
Destiny.

Texas When it Rains

There is no place quite like Texas when it rains.
The old folks already know from their aches and
    their pains
Long before the clouds even knew;
Rolling cotton pillows on a featherbed of blue.
The birds somehow seem to know too.
They abandon their heights and fly where they hide
In a sweeping, graceful, low-arched glide.

The wind from the South now shifts all around
And the smoke breaks off even and hangs near the
    ground,
The cattle in unison face the new wind,
And the fish rise to feed in a silvery flash
Sounding the water with a quick sudden splash,
While the leaves curl their edges and show their silk
    underpants.
Like Arabian harem girls when they dance.

The cicadas slow their relentless song.
You almost miss them when the racket is gone.
The clouds boil up in black anvil tops,
And the smell of roots and earth and grass
Fills the atmosphere with intoxicating gas.
Rumbles and murmurs of rumors to come
Sound on the prairie like a far-away drum.

Then one icy drop, then three; ten, then twenty
Dripping so fast and dropping so many
You never can count them all as they fall.
If you've paid attention and got your fly tied up
    right
You can sit back and pack your old briar tight
And listen as raindrops play your canvas all night
Composing music only The Master could write.

Well, it might just blow over, but it may just get
    worse.
What started as a blessing could end up a curse.
The clouds turn yellow and purple and green
Like a big ugly bruise on the back of your hand.
The wind and the lightning can wreak havoc on the
    land.
But it always begins with such sweet, sweet
    refrains.
There is no place quite like Texas when it rains.

Hill Country

The land lifts and falls but gradually slants
downward, southeast toward the gulf.
The hill country knolls, prairie-grass blessed, are
sun-kissed with wild-flower stuff.
The land at first glance, when suitably dressed, like
long-fabled lands in our dreams,
From the northern plateau to the sea down below is
really quite more than it seems.

The tableland flats pushed up by the Earth, while
forming long centuries ago,
Are slowly eroded by wind and by rain into karst
tomb-like caverns below.
Limestone cracks and faults from the strain, leaving
deep canyons and rills.
Aquifer fed springs feed cold rippled streams
draining the rocky-faced hills.

Tall yellow grass as high as your waist grew hardy
past prairie oak mott.
A place where both man and animal roamed in a
paradise time long forgot.
Where buffalo grazed past a pink granite dome;
pecan and fruit trees grew wild;
Where water was found pushed out of the ground at
a place where man was beguiled.

So quickly it changes, from a paradise found to a
desert on the edge of a lie.
When rains fail to fall and the aquifer dries up;
when the summer sun rises high.
When the grasses die brown in dreadful drought,
and the ground cracks under your feet,
Filled full of strife, it's a hard scrabble life, in the
crust and the dust and the heat.

The game moved away to follow the grass; the men
then followed the game.
What choice did they have? You go while you can,
or you die while you wait, watching the sky for the
    rain.
Rivals for water now, critter and man, crowd near
shallow seeps, once springs,
And they pray for the day when the heat gives away
to the rain that the heat often brings.

Clouds, heavy laden, are brought inland high, aloft
on the south coastal wind,
Which then hits the rim of the upland plateau, and
condenses the moisture within.
Down from the clouds to the landscape below, the
moisture now forms in drops.
Sweet, summer rain now graces the plain and also
the distant hilltops.

The cold front that triggered the life-giving rains
has stalled out over the plain.
The cold lofty air meets warm southern breezes and
creates even more rain.
It is so hard to know in times such as these, if it's a
half-full or a half-empty cup.
The rain comes so fast the ground has surpassed the
capacity to soak it all up.

From the hills high above, the water now flows into
the deep rocky canyons below.
The amount now far outpaces the need and causes
the dry streambeds to flow.
Increasing in mass as it increases speed, while the
rain continues to fall,
In a maddening dash, quick as a flash, it moves
downstream like a wall.

Now rushing full force down river and gorge, the
surge is increased by the mud.
The canyons now drum in a deafening roar, as all is
swept up in the flood.
You can hear boulders roll on the hard river floor,
as the flood expresses its wrath.
Trees that that are downed, and anything drowned,
are carried along in its path.

Water seeks its own natural level and drains itself
down to the sea.
The river of life that water provides is a lesson for
both you and for me.
The people that live and are left to survive,
somehow managed to cheat
The death that came with the life giving rain. The
irony now is complete.

The land lifts and falls but gradually slants
downward, southeast to the gulf.
The hill country knolls, prairie-grass blessed, are
sun-kissed with wild-flower stuff.
The land at first glance, when suitably dressed, like
long-fabled lands in our dreams,
From the northern plateau to the sea down below, is
really quite more than it seems.

The Mesquite Bean War

The Spirit in the Stone

Stump sitting, as rock doves peck among the clefts and cliffs,
He rocks and taps his foot to rhythms of the swirling swift
Running stream as it trickles past the peeking cypress knees;
Hearing olden sweetwater songs composed by stream and breeze,
Sung long before the men who stank of river, smoke, and sweat
From ages past in ageless time – before time was made up yet.
He spits a flume between his boots and rises from his seat
No time to listen more among the trees at nature's feet.

Too much to do! No time to sit… The light is fading fast.
The sun slips slow beneath the rim beyond the rocky crest.
The weakened yellow light now casts the palish limestone face
Into a softened, smoother stone; now fairy-light encased.

12

Down the bank from the water's edge the adept eye
detects,
Amongst the trees, some other stones the same light now
reflects.
He rolls aside rubble rocks and finds a kitchen midden
That daylight-bathed five hundred years, lay for the ages
hidden.

Here is where their campfires lay -- the smoke still
clings to trees
From a million some such campfire pits beneath the stars
and leaves.
Shell and bone long cast aside, the refuse of the sloven,
The blacked stones reveal the site of an ancient cooking
oven.

Between his callused fingers pressed, remnants of an
aged meal
Are exhumed by naked fist and examined by the feel.
At last, he finds among the shards the object of his quest
An arrow point knapped long ago, and chipped with a
moonlike crest.

With gentle fingers now withdraws an heirloom caked in
dirt.
He cleans the trophy with his spit and wipes it on his
shirt.
Small and precious in loving palm, the arrow point now
lies
That lay so long within the earth unseen by human eyes.

The moon-shaped chip made useless offal of the stone so
cold.
What before was hapless thrown away, now is held like
gold.
Long cold, it lay beneath the ground. It warms now in
his clutch.
The spirit soars within the stone responding to his touch.

The spirit-guided cause-effect engendered inspiration
Of untold tales, unvoiced woes, and unknown
tribulation.
Who drove him here to find so deep a touchstone of
regret?
To tell the tales he never knew, of those he never met?

How could he tell of such things yet, with hand so
unqualified?
How could he breathe life into a world that long ago had
died?
The spirit has its tales to tell, so with the stone in hand,
He sets for home to dream and write of an ancient far-off
land.

Without delay he hurries back to hammer on his keys.
To get down the rhyme in time before the ageless spirit
flees.
The evening sky turns swiftly now a paler shade of blue
The full moon peeks above the cliffs; while behind the
rock doves coo.

14

Son of the Wolf

Haggard, tired, and scared and hungry, on foot, he ran
for four long days.
Harassed on the trail by horse-backed warriors who
coveted his life.
He had no time to stop or eat.

Little Crow moved mainly south. Searching for the
safety of his clan.
Harsh hunger grew inside his belly like a wild and
vicious beast.
He must eat soon or die tonight.

There was no time to stop and eat. There was no place to
stop and sleep.
Between fear and need lay certainty: without food, he
would surely die.
He must make time to eat tonight.

A buffalo calf had strayed away from the safety of the
herd.
The herd grazed the hillside ahead, and there on the
hillside behind,
The calf, the lance, and Little Crow.

The calf did not see him draw near, low to the ground
and running fast.
He threw the lance, found its mark, and quickly pierced
the little heart.
Fell dead before it hit the ground.

Insane with hunger, he pounced upon the jerking, furry
form.
He forced the drooling mouth agape, and stretched a
pink wet tongue.

He sliced off slippery meat with one fast slash and ate in
two large bites.
He rolled the calf onto its back, sliced through the soft,
curly belly,
And pulled out the beating heart.

Gnawing at the steaming meat, he tilted his head and
drank.
The blood spewed down his cheeks and splashed across
his chest.
He ripped the gory stomach wide and stuck his head
inside the hole.
He lapped the warm sweetgrass milk the calf had
suckled.
The calf had been well fed.

He pulled intestines forth in bloody, long, knobby ropes,
And wound them, like a sticky snake, looped around his
neck.
He quickly stood and ran again, leaving sign of his
passing.
The buffalo cadaver still bled and steamed in the cold,
late afternoon.
Southward – ever southward.

His belly full, he fully sensed the fear rise inside his
guts.
As he ran on, with every step, pain coursed throughout
his brain.
Now fed, he knew he needed rest, but fearfully forced
himself to run.
He was a hunted, haggard thing, and knew that death
was oh! So near!
And death was unforgiving.

16

The sky grew quickly darker now. He scanned the brush
for a hiding place.
In a brushy knoll on the side of the hill, he found an oak
tree on its side.
He scooped a hole beneath the trunk.

Though on its side, it remained alive, and green, leafy
branches grew.
Screened by Agarita and cedar, he burrowed beneath
leaves and litter,
And quickly hid himself beneath.

He lay there panting, fighting sleep, as mosquitoes
buzzed his ears.
Soon he had caught his bated breath, and would now at
last get rest.
The yellow sun was sinking fast.

Little Crow lay quiet … still … like a rotting log beneath
the tree.
If he were going to get some sleep, now was the time it
had to be.
Unsure if he would wake again.

He slept a tortured, restless sleep, and dreamt of mother
and of wife.
Four days past, the evil men who ran him now, had
taken both their lives,
And raped them both within his sight.

In that awful night he had slipped away and now was a
hunted man;
Through the rock-laced prairie, they chased him four
days and nights.
Hoary hands reached out for him from the dark, and he
ran, sleeping still.

He jumped awake. The hooting owl nearby had alerted
his mind.
It was no owl. Comanche.

It was full dark now, they backtracked his sign,
searching for his trail.
He heard them close; they walked like dogs through
crunch-dried leaves.
Almost right on top of him, in the ever-growing evening
dark.
Coming from the south. He could not see them, but they
were so close.
They talked. They breathed. They stank.

They climbed and sat upon his tree; one stepped upon
his back.
They talked about the sign he left and the kill he left
behind.
There were four. From the still warm calf, they knew
that he was near.
They decided he had hidden in the grass between them
and the kill.
They were going to make a camp.

They chose a guard. The other three would go to get the
calf.
They believed that when the sun rose up, their prey
would run again.
When he ran past this very point, they would spring their
ambush plan.
The plot was good, except that he was not where they
thought he was.
He was right beneath them all.

Three rode away, while one man watched and climbed
the log above.
The moon showed signs of rising soon, to light his
hiding place.
Any moment he might be discovered.

He could not see the man who sat above him in the
darkened light.
He recognized the leggings and the moccasins of the
fiend above.
In the full moonlight, he would be found.

Surely soon they would quickly rush back with carcass
of calf in tow.
They would take the meat to the nearby creek and cook
it for their meal.
Maybe, then, he could slip away.

He heard the man above him grunt, pulling leaves from
the live oak tree.
He smelled the stink, and felt the drop in the middle of
his back.
They would not look too closely now.

The man leapt from the log as the rising moon peeked
above the horizon.
Comanche brave crouched upon a rock, watching,
waiting, and listening.
Soon it would be his time to die.

The yellow moon, so big and bright, grew larger in the
sky.
Impossibly large, and more fearfully bright than he had
ever seen.
He held his breath, hoped the rising moon would not
reveal his place.

The moon swept the eastern sky. The guard kept silent
standing watch.
Little Crow crawled from his hole.

The Comanche brave was a silhouette inside the full
faced moon.
The shadow dropped the lance, bow, and shield onto the
ground.
In the shadows, Little Crow could hear the piss against
the flat hard rock.
Crow rose up from his hiding place and sent an arrow
into his neck.
Dead before he hit the ground.

He pounced upon the flailing man, and cut his belly
wide.
Through spewing blood, Crow spilled the gory guts onto
the ground.
For the second time this very night, he ripped a heart
from a warm body,
Held the still-warm heart to the moon, and howled his
victory scream.
Tonkawa! Son of the Wolf!

He grasped the dead man's hair and pulled it back from
off the neck.
He gashed the scalp from ear to ear and cut across the
forehead.
He tightly seized bloody flap and tore the scalp from
dead man's head.
He could not proudly go into the afterlife without hair.
Denied the spirit world.

Next he pulled the dead man's tongue, stretched it out,
and sliced if off.
Now he could not brag or sing of his worldly deeds on
the other side.
He threw the tongue into the brush.

He danced around the lifeless form, whirling the scalp
around his head.
Blood from the gory relic splayed out in a large circle
around the body.
He tucked the scalp into his waist.

He screamed aloud to the yellow moon in exulted
celebration!
Stopping his dance, he knelt again by the despised
Comanche body.
There was one last thing that he must do.

He grasped the dead man's organs in his bloody hand
and quickly cut.
Sliced them off and threw them in the brush for brother
wolves to eat.
He would rape no more, forever.

Fed and rested, and now avenged, he knew escape was
in his hand.
He mounted the dead man's horse, grabbed its mane,
and rode away.
Southward – ever southward.

Epilogue:

Have you known hunger, not just a missed meal or two,
or a day or two?
Have you felt the beast gnawing in your belly eating you
from inside?
Have you stood on the verge of starvation, and known
you were dying?
Have your bowels stopped moving because you had
nothing to process?
Have you felt your strength ebb, as you stood on the
brink of death?

If you were that hungry,
Would you kill a buffalo calf and eat its raw tongue?
Would you drink its blood, and devour the tender heart
muscle?
Would you consume the sweetgrass mother's milk inside
its stomach?
Would you call savage, one who did?

Have you known exhaustion, not just fatigue or tired
from work?
Have you run four days, fleeing death, stopping only
moments at a time?
Have you felt the ache in your side and legs as you ran
against the wind?
Have you stopped to retch into the nearby bushes?
Have you dry-heaved the black, bitter bile from your
empty stomach?

If you were that tired,
Would you dig a hole and try to hide in the filthy, musty
smelling earth?
Would you lie death-like in fear as mosquitoes swarmed
you face?

Could you quiet terrors in your head, unknowing if you
would reawake?
Would you call savage, one who did?

Have you known fear, not just scared, not just the
thought you might die?
Have you known your killer would mutilate you while
you still lived?
Have you realized that a lesser man could snuff out your
life?
Have you known with all your heart that life is not fair
and no one cares?
Have you discovered that it does not matter anyway?

If you were that fearful,
Would you lie deathly quietly as your enemy covered
you in excrement?
Would you stop your very breath for fear of fatal
discovery?
Would you hide like an animal in the dirt and filth?
Would you call savage, one who did?

Have you known anger – not just annoyance – not just
irritation?
Have you felt fury rise within your belly and take control
of your soul?
Have you felt the vehemence and heat of wrath?
Have you gone blind with rage?
Have you felt the passion and the thirst for revenge?

If you were that angry,
Would you take the life of another man?
Would you rip out his tongue and his still-beating heart?
Would you take his scalp so he could not enter the after-
life?
Would you call savage, one who did?

Have you known joy – not just happy – not just pleased?
Have you danced in glee at being alive despite
insurmountable odds?
Have you sung in celebration your victory at the hands
fortune and fate?
Have you bathed in the warm blood of the weaker
defeated?
Have you delighted in the knowledge that it was not
your blood?

If you were that joyful,
Would you dance in the moonlight in joyous
celebration?
Would you scream to the moon in the elation of still
being alive?
Would you castrate he who raped and killed your mother
and sister?
Would you call savage, one who did?

Would you live, or
Would you die?

Would you spare the calf or the man?

Song of Sonora

Below the fractured, faulted rock that men now call
Balcones,
Lived a breed of men before the days of guns and
ponies.
South along the river bends, and out along the coastal
plains,
Lie swampy lands, where men eat men, and feast upon
their brains.

To the west, there lies a rock-strewn place, cactus filled
and dry,
Where ragged wind sweeps past big bend, and
mountains meet the sky.
With gleaming heads and riding beasts, came
Conquistadores.
With murderous haste, they crossed the place they call
the Great Sonora.

The silvered cities lost, then found, then sacked, then
lost again,
The fables old of streets of gold have cost ten-thousand
men.
They left behind the bloody brush along those dry
stream courses.
They left their tales on dusty trails; and left behind wild
horses!

Though dry most times, and water sparse, there are times
when it rains,
When freighter clouds float darkened skies, up from the
coastal plains.
The desert drinks like a man who cannot hold his liquor;
When it rains at last – it drinks as fast, but the desert
dries out quicker.

Dry and parched a day past rain; so where does the water
go?
It leaves behind a wondrous sign where a billion
blossoms grow.
The water seeps beneath cracked rock, or gathers up in
streams
And comes out slow in a silvered flow below San
Marcos springs.

Stronger bands stole Tonkawa lands on the prairies far
up north.
Homeless Tonkawa – pushed away by those who rode
the horse.
Following the great bison herds that, too, were harassed
south,
The sons of wolves had no recourse but to live there
hand to mouth.

They found at last a place serene where spirit water sings
And peaceful lived a hundred years below the shady
springs.
They gathered nuts and tanned their hides, and tried to
live despite,
The callous stride and ruthless tide of ever-spreading
whites.

The Germans came, but never knew; the gringos knew
much less!
With barking guns, the Rangers pushed the lowly
Tonkawa west.
Through jagged, faulted, Balcones and up a rocky draw,
Until Comanche saw their smoke, and killed or captured
all.

The men they slew – the old ones too! They slaved or
raped the rest.
Their bastard sons, they left to die upon Great Sonora's
breast.
Apache west; Comanche north; and caught between the
three
Between white and right, and red and wrong, the
Tonkawa ceased to be.

The stragglers joined the white man's cause to try to
right the wrong,
But, no amount of loyalty could change the red man's
song.
And in the end, it counted naught, and for their
preservation,
White man moved the red man north to a homeless
reservation.

But out along those desert trails, on darkened desert
nights,
If you know just where to watch, you may see their spirit
lights.
Out there past Pisano Pass – on the great and vast
Sonora –
Bleached bones glow white in pale moonlight, among
Conquistadores.

Where the Wild Rice Grows

Down within the valley, where the wild rice grows,
Alongside the river, where the cold spring flows,
In search of the herd and in search of the nuts,
Across the rocky desert, we dragged our huts.
We hid from our troubles and we eased our weary woes,
And made our home by the river, where the wild rice
grows.

Without any weapons but the lethal lance and bow
We stalked the antlered elk and we killed the buffalo.
Pushed from the high plains, in olden days long past
We scrabbled for a hard life, and we lived it hard and
fast.
Driven from the prairie by our fears and by our foes,
We made a home by the river, where the wild rice
grows.

Hiding from Comanche and the brutal, wild, Waco
The sons of wolves live lives of peace among the fawns
and doe.
In the peaceful, shady, valley 'neath the tall and splendid
trees
We live a life of pleasure, and we live a life of ease.
Where we live tomorrow, only the haunted wind knows.
Today, our home is by the river, where the wild rice
grows.

We gather flint rock gravel to point the long arrows;
We harvest nuts and mesquite to trade with caballeros.

We trade with fierce Apaches and the strange Mescalero.
We get what we can, and take what we get, all with
limbered bow.
We trade with our fiercest enemies as well as our amigos
Down by the river, where the wild rice grows.

Out past the windswept hills onto the flattened far
plateaus,
Where the sun bakes the hardpan ground and waterless
arroyos,
You can see the signs of battle; you can see the mighty
flood
Of the white man's unrelenting letting of the red man's
blood.
Here, all is peace and quiet, in the grassy, sweet
meadows.
In our home along the river, where the wild rice grows.

If you go down farther south, toward the tongue of
Mexico
You can hear the echoed thunder among the old pueblos.
According to the educated views of ancient Mexicans
Only fools could ever trust the word of the Texicans.
We make our home between the Mex and the strange
gringos.
Here, along the river, where the wild rice grows.

Caught between the ages and the stages nature throws,
We tightly hold our clan together and we keep upon our
toes.
We do not want to fight again and we are far too tired to
run.

We cannot hope to defend ourselves without the horse or
gun.
Caught here, like a hounded hare, in this tranquil home
we chose.
Here, along the river, where the wild rice grows.

If we could know our future and plan all our great
tomorrows,
We would have us all live together forever, here in the
cool shadows.
Together we would smoke and eat, and we would share
a happy dance
And sing of our great fortune, and we would never take a
chance
On losing the peaceful life we have found beneath these
misty rainbows.
Here, along the river, where the wild rice grows.

For what could we possibility gain by coming such to
blows?
What ill could be so terrible that we must fiercely rise to
oppose?
Cannot we live in peace and harmony, secure in sacred
trust?
Why must we main and kill each other, just to satisfy our
lust?
We have a land of plenty, cannot we share it friends and
foes.
Here, along the river, where the wild rice grows?

Buffalo Dreams

My son, last night I dreamed the clover bloomed.
The white blossoms spread across the prairie like pale skin
On the wide rocky valley beyond Llano –
The Llano our ancestors, the Chianas, named
Before even our mother's fathers were born.

The sweet smell of clover lifted high above
To blow with warm winds to the far places.
The scent was so tempting and so alluring
That it seduced the great, hooved, hairy animals,
The buffalo that once we hunted free.

Buffalo returned, to graze again within
The great, wide Valley of the Chianas.
In droves they came, across the blossomed plain.
Their rumble woke us as we lay sleeping.
We grabbed our bows and spears, and ran to see.

We danced the dance of the buffalo once more!
We painted faces bright, and smeared our limbs
With the last of the precious ochre-colored oils.
First, we gave thanks for our great providence.
And praised the hairy beasts that gave us meat.

Oh, mighty buffalo! Where have you strayed?

Why have you left your people for so long?
Were we not, then, grateful enough for you?
Did we not give our thanks for your bounty?
Did we forget to make some sacred rite?

More importantly, why have you now returned?
Have you come back to stay forever now?
Oh! We have missed you much, and praise you even
more.
You have blessed us with your presence in our time.
Feed us, clothe us, and house us once again.

Cure our sick and dying; provide our fires;
Give us bone for tools, and we shall honor you.
It shall again be of old, when you were here.
We respectfully accept your generous offer,
And grieve for you, even as we celebrate your death.

After we had danced and prayed, my son,
We took our weapons and went to claim our prize.
And you were also there, my pride, with me!
On hands and knees, we crept the fragrant grass
And quietly gathered on the hilltop there.

Look out across the river valley wide.
Far more than we could count! They grazed for miles.
We could smell their stench soar on the warm soft
breeze,
We knew the same wind carried our smell too.
Above, slow moving clouds eclipsed the moon.

We used the cover of the dark to move.
On hands and knees, we silent crept so near.
Swiftly we were among them in the dark.

We could hear them moving in the tall, high grass.
Waiting, as bloodlike red streaked the sky,

We swatted gnats and flies drawn by their dung.
When it was time, we quickly rose and stood.
We began to see the trees – the rocks – bunch grass.
We saw everything – but the buffalo!
We fired the dry ocotillo, but they were gone

Like a laughing specter, they had disappeared.
Awake now, I realized it was but a dream.
I was so sad! I wanted it to be,
But it was not, and I was left a fool.
I know the buffalo are gone for good!

Brought to their knees, their hairy bodies lie
Among the bones with our fathers in the far north.
Wasted by the white men, who, with their guns,
Killed them all beneath the merciless sun,
Left their bones to be picked clean by the carrion eaters.

The shooting did not stop until all were dead,
And, like our dreams, they rotted upon the earth.

Far Flung Tales

Glyfada Square

To Glyfada Square from the shadow of Mars,
The lights of Athens shine beneath ancient stars.
Dionysus reigns in festive air
And the whole world sings
In Glyfada Square.

At Piraeus each day where the ships come in
With Lira and Franks and Marks and men,
But neither Paris, nor Rome, nor even Venice
compare
To the beauty and warmth
In Glyfada Square.

Did Diogenes look with his lantern bright
Across the plain in broad daylight?
Did he search in vain and die in despair?
Did his lantern shine
In Glyfada Square?

Years have passed and I've gone my way.
I've traveled far. But, on certain days
My mind goes back to that place so fair.
My heart still yearns
For Glyfada Square.

Featured as the poet of the week on Writer's Haven
VerseLand 9/21/14

Donne Vecchia

Donne Vecchia dressed in black from head down to their

toes.

Warm shawls wrapped around the back from the cold

wind that blows.

Bent at waist, they stooped and squat; they forage the

grass for snails

To add to the evening pasta pot, and drop them in their

pails.

I wonder what their thoughts reveal, these matrons

dressed in black?

Is it only the lumache meal, or do their memories

wander back

To days gone by; when love was new, before the black

took hold?

Before life drained the color from their lives; black

dominoes against a

      sky of gold.

Did they forsake color for a reason, a season, or a loss of

youthful years?

Or, do they wear the darker shade because it hides their

tears?

We know that black will hold the heat from Mother

Nature's sun,

But maybe, simply, it's just because, it's what they've

always done.

*Featured as the poet of the week on Writer's Haven
VerseLand 9/21/14*

Mexicali Pickup

Down in Mexicali where the coyotes run
Known as the city that captured the sun
Fly too close and you're gonna get a burn
You'd think by now they would learn.
Some of them just never gonna learn.

Only hot air stirring from that electric fan
Try to stay cool any way you can

Too hot for coffee; too early for beer
Got to get some air in here.
Need some fresh air in here.

Throw open the door and the windows wide
A little bit of breeze blows the curtain inside
Then it sucks it back out just as fast as it came
Wonder if it's ever gonna rain?
Lord, we sure need some rain.

Little kids out walking to school with their books
Giving each other such mischievous looks
Laughter echoes off the walls as they play
It's good to be young that way.
So good to be young that way. (You wish they
could stay that way)

Sun so hot, it is melting the street
Hot tar burning their little toes and feet
Jumping from shade to shade to shade
This is the day the Lord has made.
Singing, this is the day that the Lord has made.

Traffic has been honking since just before dawn
Shirt's already sweaty before you put it on
Up a little alley, someone's singing a song
Passersby are singing along.
Everyone is singing along.

Senora has a face that would stop a clock
But she's got a heart of gold, and a steaming pot.
Wraps a tortilla around some mystery meat.
It's good to have something to eat.

She always has good tacos to eat.

High heels tapping on cement walk.
Secretary in a hurry; no time to talk.
She wouldn't stop to talk to a gringo anyway.
We wouldn't have a whole lot to say.
Probably not a lot we could say.

Cross the cobbled street to the shady side.
Wait there in the shadows for a taxi ride.
Take me to the airport the quickest way.
I gotta pick up my package today.
I'm picking up my package today.

A group of men standing on the hot tarmac
Near a federale cruiser with a man in the back.
They snap a police handcuff onto my left hand.
The other end they hook to the man.
On the other end, is a mighty bad man.

One behind the other we climb on the plane.
I show him my badge, and I tell him my name.
He don't want to talk, so we'll keep it that way.
We wouldn't have a whole lot to say.
Probably not a lot we could say.

Mexico is sinking as the plane starts to rise.
View outside the window has the sun in our eyes.
Fly too close and you're gonna get a burn.
You'd think by now they would learn.

Some of them just never gonna learn.

Newfie Girl

She was just a little Newfie girl, maybe five but not
much more.
She lived beside the icy sea, on the coast of Labrador.
Her father fished, her mother cried and ran the traps each
day.
Things were thin for the fishermen and worsened every
day.

They lived in a run-down shanty back in the woods
outside of town
Because he drank the monthly rent each night when the
sun went down.
The little girl would come each day to knock upon our
door.
With Inuit and pidgin talk, she called herself Lenore.

She had hair as black as the midnight sky, and eyes
bright as a star.
And when she laughed it sounded just like sweet music
from afar.
She'd come inside, and sit and watch, as quiet as a little
mouse.
And marvel at all the things she saw, we had inside our
house.

We had no children of our own, and she was very sweet.
And every day my wife would make a treat for her to
eat.
And, oh! The look that came on her face; you could tell
she loved it so!
It gave us joy to sit and play with our own little Eskimo.

We slowly grew even more attached; she came nearly
every day.

And as her grasp of English grew, she had even more to
say.
She taught us much of the frozen North; the stories she
could tell!
We taught her songs and little poems, and bible verse as
well.

The days grew short, the mercury dropped, and the snow
began to fall.
The cold snow banks outside our door were already six
feet tall.
The time had come for my wife to leave before she got
socked in.
And I would stay on the cold DEW line, with all the
other men.

Then, near the end, she came again, and to our great
delight
She told us that her mother would give birth that very
night.
Oh! How exciting it must be – to have a newborn child!
But little Lenore seemed quite concerned, and sat and
never smiled.

We thought it was perhaps because my wife was going
to go away.
So she asked Lenore about the child when she came
around next day.
"It was a girl," she solemnly said. "Another mouth to
feed."
'Paqujait." Was all she would say – the law they all must
heed.

When I got home that afternoon, the wife was going
wild.
Forget the law! No matter what, we must try to save that

child!
How could a man be so cruel, no matter how much he
drank?
To leave a newborn child to die and freeze in a cold
snow bank?

We trudged our way to their lonely shack through a crust
of icy snow.
The red-streaked sky was just a dot, where the sun was
supposed to go.
When we got there, the house was dark, not even the
dogs around.
Her father had moved them farther north, so they could
not be found!

We searched all night until my watch announced a brand
new day.
We poked through every snowbank from Happy Valley
to Goose Bay!
We did not find that baby girl; I guess we were too late.
The last plane south was leaving base, and it would just
not wait.

The wife went away, the snows came on, and the sun did
not get high.
Every night I watched Aurora Borealis crawl the
midnight sky.
Thank God, I don't have a choice like that! It makes you
catch your
          breath!
To have to watch your baby die or your family starve to
death.

I never saw Lenore again, but I once heard someone say
The family moved to Newfoundland, to fish on St.
John's Bay.

I sometimes think of that little babe, and wonder about Lenore,
Who lived beside the icy sea, on the coast of Labrador.

> **Jump up** Bower, Bruce (1994-11-26). "Female infanticide: northern exposure – Intuit may have killed one out of every five female babies between 1880 and 1940." www.Findarticles.com. Retrieved 2011-01-24.

The Caravan

Once I knelt, as if in a dream, in a strange and mystic land,
And scoured my dish in a misty stream with Turkish river sand.
A tinkle sound floated beneath the murky morning fog,
And I wondered if it were a goat, or perhaps a shepherd's dog.
The lemon blossomed air perfumed the Anatolian nights.
I was up before the dawn beneath the Tarsus heights.
The stream was cold and running free, as was my enchanted mind

42

When I heard sudden other sounds coming from behind.

Now, bandits lurk within the rocks, and travelers must
beware.
I dropped my pan, grabbed my staff, and stood with
shoulders square.
There! I heard it again just now! Was that a cock that
crowed?
Someone, or surely something, was coming down that
road!
Ding… ding… ding. The little bells tinkled with every
step it took.
With no escape, I stood there trapped, with back against
the brook.

Then at last there suddenly appeared a black and gnarly
dog.
And, eight feet high, a dromedary emerged from the
swirling fog.
Draped around the camel's neck were plaited ropes of
vibrant color.
And close behind, another came – and then there came
another!
Draped in black with golden braids, a master astride his
gangly ride,
And surveyed the world that passed below, erect and
dignified.

Their bodies draped in darkened shapes from the cloaks
that were worn,
And silver bridles were held in hands that glittering
jewels adorned.
First came the men riding high, with long, crooked
knives at side,
Pitching back and forth to match the awkward gait of the
camel's stride.

Then came camels without a rider, but packed high with
bundled loads
Of provisions, supplies, necessities, and all their
household goods

After that, the ducks and fowl and laying hens were
stowed,
And in a single cage high atop, was the rooster that had
crowed.
Then came the children that were old enough to sit a
camel's back.
In single file, they rode along. Three or four deep they
were stacked.
Close behind came the oxen, cattle, sheep, and mules.
Linked by ropes they followed close, burdened down
with tools.

The last to come, following close behind the family
cattle,
Came the women of the clan, bringing up the rear like
chattel.
But, oh! What chattel these women were! With gowns of
silver threads,
And gold and beads, and dazzling jewels draped from
covered heads.
Golden coins wound around each waist, and boots of the
finest fleece,
And feathers and furs of exotic game adorned each and
every piece.

I watched enthralled, as one by one, they marched past

me where I stood.
I realized this camel train held everything they owned.
Where were they going? How far had they come? It was
all a mystery.
But I felt the luckiest man on earth, to witness this
parade of history.

Was it a dream? Or, was it real? Sometimes, it seems too
grand.
That I witnessed a caravan of life in a strange and mystic
land.
Out of time and out of place, I stood awed, with staff in
hand,
And marveled beside a babbling brook, on Turkish river
sand.

Deep Water Runs Still

Life Cycle

Deep within the human cell
Where life and death go on,
Some say cells begin to die
When the will to live is gone.

Others claim that cells decay,
There in close proximity,
To internal schedules.
Lapse of time - eternity.

Another view, held by some
Scientists who ought to
know;

Chains of common error start
That end in death's final
blow.

The building blocks of
humankind

Live and die by supreme
laws.

As the final product wrought,
Cannot man, himself, find
cause?

Or, is it hopelessly clear
That nothing can now unlock
The secrets to survival
Chained to a relentless clock?

Or, is error-catastrophe,
With all mankind at stake
The last destiny of man?
Accumulation of mistake?

Sermon in Azure Blue
(Church Night in the Park)

The young boy knelt there on his knees
Beneath the Texas Live Oak trees.
As we listened to the preacher talk,
He sketched out a cross in sidewalk chalk.
Much larger than himself, he slowly drew
A vacant, hollow cross is azure blue.

Next to the cross there on the ground,
He drew a stick-figure man who walked
around.
He drew on a head of monstrous size,
And colored in the nose and eyes.
Then, when he had rested for a little while,
Drew on that face a gigantic smile.

I wondered who the boy had drawn,
As the preacher continued on and on;

Maybe himself or perhaps his Dad.
Whoever it was, he was surely glad!
Then he drew a box above the frame,
And labeled in there Jesus' name.

Holy Father! Full of Grace!
A smile upon the Jesus face?
What is this young world coming to?
A sacrilege in azure blue!
But the more I looked, the more I saw.
This picture was not so wrong at all.

      And finally did I realize,
      This boy had drawn our Christ alive!
      Not nailed upon the cross in pain,
      But walking around; not hung in
shame
      But glorified in victory!
      That is what his picture said to me.

      How would you prefer to see
      Our precious Jesus and that tree?
      Hung in pain and misery,
      Or walking around for all to see?
      Smiling as if the beat the band!
      And all this from a young boy's
hand.

A testament from an innocent view,
In sidewalk chalk in azure blue.

Photographs

Photographs that line the wall
Tell of memories to recall;
Tell of moments meant to keep;
Tell of mobile memorabilia fleet.

The intended meaning is very clear
To he who held the moment dear.
No one else would sing sublime.
How else to photograph a time?

And, once the times have passed
along,

With no one left to sing their song,
Of what use are these memographs?
Become then, mere photographs.

Photographs to line the wall.
Perhaps to hide a blemish small.
Or, because they always hung there
before.

Artful sentries beside the door.

But, they hang a little lower station
Reduced to mere decoration.
Yet, the secrets hide there all the
same.

Obscured by photograph, glass, and
frame.

My Resume

The director looked up from his score
And said, "What all have you played
before?"
The lights were hot, and the stage was bare.
I fixed him with a focused stare.
"Soldier, scholar
Husband, father
Singer, writer,
Quitter, fighter and rainbow rider.
Worker, boss,
Newly found,
And completely lost.
Good old boy, saintly sinner,
Practiced hand, and rank beginner.
Teacher, preacher,
Lovable loser, and over-reacher.

All these I've played,
And even more,

From coast to coast and shore to shore.
And never once have I ever dropped a line,
Or failed to show for a role of mine."

The director stood and said at last,
"Tell all the others the role is cast! "

The Teacher's Bouquet

Flowers grow along the lane
Where once was only grass and weed.
And, with tender care and rain,
It was I, who supplied their urgent need.

They came to me un-blossomed shoots.
Within, their sheltered seeds did lie.
Knowledge poured upon their roots
So that someday they might grow high.

Grow, they did. Now dawns the day
When long awaited buds appear.
I await the new-crop spray,
With slate cleaned for the coming year.

The Rest is up to Him

If I've touched one and helped him grow
Then I'll be glad, because I'll know
I've done my part to make him whole.
The rest is up to him.

And, if someday, alone he stands,
And keeps his feet on shifting sands,
He'll walk alone from loving hands.
The rest is up to Him.

Love and Life and Oranges

Come sit with me a little while,
And for the price of just one smile
I'll tell you all I ever knew
of love, and life, and all things true.

You see this orange? It has no rhyme.
Bitter and pungent is its rind.
But the juice inside is heavenly sweet

and so is all the pulpy meat.

But if you let it sit too long, well then
it gets brown spots on its skin.
It sort of slumps and gets out of round;
Falls off the tree onto the ground.

But pluck it while it's ripe and sweet.
Treasure each one as a special treat.
Hold to it tight. Not too loose!
Squeeze out every drop of juice.

Suck it hard until it's dried.
Eat all the fleshy fruit inside.
Then, throw the dry, bitter husk away,
and save the seeds for another day.

What's that? Love and life? Oh yes!
I don't know much about those things, I
guess.
I have only one thing to say, my dear.
The more you listen, the more you hear.

The Canyon

Forsaken. Lost. Hopeless. Forlorn
Where the wind howls secrets from midnight to

morn;
Where names don't matter and the past is the past;
Where the nameless go finally to live out their last;
Where time doesn't matter and the future won't
hold.
The damned sleep restless in the canyon so cold.

They cover their sins with slumber, and yet
They sleep to remember, and dream to forget.
They huddle in fear and shiver with fright.
They walk the empty canyon each night.
No one knows why; even they cannot say;
Searching for something they lost on the way.

It don't matter much if you get up or stay down
At least you can't fall when you're flat on the
ground.
The walls are too steep to climb out anyway.
Escaping is hopeless. You can't get away.
And where would you go on your short, aimless
jaunts?
The canyon will keep what no one else wants.

What is left of your hope when nothing sustains?
Not even the dope you shoot in your veins:
Neither the smoke you blow to the wind,
Nor even the wine that takes you back … there
again.
Back to the life, you now only know in your sleep
Before you got lost in the canyon so deep.

So, you abandon all hope; you don't even try.
You are too tired to die, and you're too sad to cry.
In your misery and pain, it is so hard to see
That death is not the only way to be free.
Has nobody told you? Have you not heard?
Have you forgotten the promise in His word?

You don't have to stand up, just get to your knees.
You will find that you are loved despite your
disease.
You will run without tiring, you will walk and not
fall.
As on wings of the eagles, you'll fly over the wall.
You'll rise from the canyon and stand there in awe
Of the Creator, Redeemer, and Master of all.

Who has measured the waters in the cup of His
hand,
And meted out heaven in one single span?
Who has considered the earth and the dust without
fail,
And used mountains and hills to balance the scale?
When you've reached rock bottom you'll find one
thing is true,
The only one keeping you in the canyon ...
Is you.

Isaiah 40

The Pines

The
Pines,
Stately,
Tall and green.
Evergreen, linear,
Elevated, they stand,
Majestic and streamlined.
Pointers to heaven,
Totem, telegraph,

telephone,

    Tower tall. Skyscraper

trees.

    They seine the clouds and catch

the wind.

    They touch the sun and

cast

    Soft shadow, sallow,

shallow, shade.

    Carpet maker trees. Singers of

songs that sway

    To their own music.
Perfumers
Of the
Forest.

Life is Funny That Way

Al Capone and the Jaws of Death

Al Capone was all alone upon a fence of wood,
Sharpening claws and licking paws just like a good
cat should.
While far below, an Eskimo Husky was consumed
in lustful love
For a heated hound behind the fence, unmindful the
cat above.

Men oft times relate how fickle fate can pluck you
up so clean
To drop you in the path of the jaws of wrath. Life
can be so mean!
And so it was with that ball of fuzz, aloof, and safe,
and sound.
'Till a neighborhood brat plucked that cat and
tossed him on the ground.

Now the Eskimo dog was all agog, distracted as it
were.

Between the mutt and the eager slut dropped a
harried hunk of fur.
Until these events, the wooden fence was all that
barred his prize.
Now this ball of fur would steal the cur from right
before his eyes.

I was working hard in my yard, mowing by the gate.
I fought off the dog with a fireplace log before it
was too late.
Al was placed with greatest haste on a lawn mower
ambulance.
Across bumpy ground was tossed around without a
backward glance.

To the Vet we sped with Al half dead, and to the
Lord we call
For his life to spare. But, unprepared we were for
what we saw!
A hospital for pets. Without regrets we hurried forth
with pain
And entered into a twilight zone of techno-
veterinarian gain.

"Who ever heard? How absurd! I-V for a cat?" Oh!
Such urgency!
Stat! For a short-haired cat?! Exploratory
surgery???!!!

I held up my hands, refused CAT scans and
answered with a moan.
I'd be the man who took a stand and pulled the plug
on Al Capone!

So Al Capone was on his own (You need not fear
the worst.)
For ever since he has walked the fence without care
for safety first.
The Alaska hound went to the pound his would-be
mate grew cold.
And Al Capone is safe at home, and remains forever
bold.

But on certain days when in other ways he seems
normal otherwise
He'll hunker down and turn a around with a wild
look in his eyes.
He'll start to wail and swish his tail when I open the
tool shed
          door!
Hell hath no fury like Al Capone when I start that
old lawn mower!

Don't Cut My Agarita

Don't cut my Agarita. You can cut that thistle
down.
You can slash and burn those Cockleburs; that
Spurge has done turned brown.
You can pulverize that Ragweed plant; you can
chop that old Horehound.
You can kill every Cedar tree you see and hack it to
the ground.
But whatever you do, make sure that you
Don't cut my Agarita.

That Mexican Persimmon tree, you can let that one
alone to thrive.
But that Poison Ivy around the trunk; we can't let
that survive!
If you don't get a handle on that Lantana, it'll eat
your yard alive!
Get to the root of the Wild Tobacco shoot, or it
surely will revive.
But whatever you do, make sure that you
Don't cut my Agarita.

Don't get too close to the Prickly Pears or you'll be
stinging until the dawn.
I guess we don't need that Milkweed plant now that
the butterflies are gone.
That Witch's Taper Mullen plant, you can let that
thing live on.

And, those Mexican Sombreros look real pretty out
on the lawn.
**But whatever you do, make sure that you
Don't cut my Agarita!**

Let me drop a dime on you one more time, and be
sure you don't decline!
DON'T CUT MY AGARITA! It makes some
darned good wine!

My Masterpiece

Ripped from deep within my very soul
    It erupted, shrieking, from my pen
    And splashed uncorrupted across the page.
    No, not muse, or even conscious thought,
    Nor ruse; it stood and spoke, alone.
    It lived!

Somewhere it resides in some manila folder
    Deep in a pile of some teacher's
    forty years of toil,
    With C minus in red lead pencil
    Scrawled across the top.

    But, I kept a copy.

It also owns the unique distinction
    Of having been rejected
    By every major magazine
    Publisher in North America.

    But, I kept a copy.

Finally, it appeared on page four
    Of my local, home town news.
    (Cost me twenty-seven dollars and forty-
three cents.)
    It now lines the bottom of the cages
    Of the best read parakeets in town.

But, I kept a copy.

Winner, Lynne Elliot Award, Greater New Braunfels Arts Council, April 2014

Silver Belt Buckle

Well, I've got a belt with a silver buckle.
You know, that thing gives me all kinds of trouble,
Like a wild-eyed bronc loaded in a buckin' chute.
I don't like to make it sound like I'm braggin',
But a silver belt buckle is a woman magnet,
And that dang belt buckle, keeps me in trouble with
you.

I'm down at the bar with an arm load of trouble.
She's working real hard trying to shine my buckle.
Her old man walks by; gives me one of those old
evil grins.
I spun her around and I thought I'd dip her,
The buckle came lose and it stuck in her zipper!
That dang belt buckle done got me in trouble again.

Oh, it might be my smile; it could be my jeans;
Maybe it's the package – whatever that means!
I don't believe none of that any more than you do.
I'll bet my boots I'm a little to bold.
Gonna have to give up that old rodeo road
And hang up this buckle; stay out of trouble with
you.

Coco Puff

You laughed when I told you Coco was bipolar,
But she really is quite insane.
I know of no other cat even droller.
God only knows what goes on in her brain.

Hair as back as four in the morning,
Eyes as green as Chinese jade.
Purrs one moment, then turns without warning
And howls like a banshee at some movement you made

Or some slight you didn't intend,
Or maybe some inaccessible itch.
I don't understand or even pretend.
Even my sweet wife calls her a bitch.

Sometimes she sits herself on the stairs.
No one goes up, and no one goes down.
Protector or warden? Who's splitting hairs?
There's never a dull moment when Coco's around.

You try to edge past, but nothing will move her.
You speak softly and calmly while making amends.
But, all hell breaks loose when try to step over
That's when the growling and spitting begins.

Then suddenly it's over as quick as it begins.
She beats a hasty retreat.
Half an hour later, she's rubbing your shins
And begging for a kitty-cat treat.

Lord help you if the package is bare!
If you forgot to pick up supplies.
No way in hell you're getting down those stairs
When she gets that wild look in her eyes.

Dealing with Coco had gotten quite tricky.
I'm really fed up with her antics.
What would happen if I slipped her a mickey
Or laced her meow mix with some Xanax?

I'd Rather

I'd rather you told me you hated my lines

Than to nod your head and walk away.
I'd rather you told me to give up writing forever!
The truth is less painful sometimes.
I'd rather you told me to burn it all today
Than to smile and tell me, "That's a winner!"
I'd rather you said I should shoot myself dead
Than to listen and ask, "What's for dinner?"

It's not your approval I need.
It's not your praise I'm after.
It's not toward your mind I'm aiming,
It's your heart I'm wanting to feed.
It's the touch, the feeling, the pathos.
Logos and ethos be deuced!
I want it to be something you feel deep inside
Rather than something you somehow deduced.

I want you to feel me; to know where I've been:

Whether happy, or sad, or in pain.
I want you to share that, in your own memory.
I want to take you back there again.

And once there, from the distance of time
You will learn from that moment, and grow.
If you're moved, I'll know how good was my
rhyme –
I'll see it in your eyes, and I'll know.

Inside Cat

Inside cat went walking around, nosing near
and far.
Came into the dining room and found a door
ajar.
Ventured out onto the porch to see what was
all out there.
Arched her back, walked sideways, and
ruffled up her hair.

Felt the warmth of sunshine on her coat and
the heat of a yellow sun.
Saw vast lawns of verdant green and acres
there to run.
Saw feathered lunches in the sky, singing
songs of glee.
Butterflies went flitting by so happy to be
free.

Smelled the unrefrigerated air, and scents
she didn't know
Touched her nose to a big red rose, felt the
summer breezes blow.
Heard the squirrels in the trees give their
"cat on the back porch" cry.
Saw the flutter of flickering leaves beneath a
cotton candy sky.

Marveled at the paradise outside where she
had never been

Didn't like it.

Came back in.

I Came to Watch You Die

He walked right in like he owned the place, and got right down
      here in my face.
He smelled like barn and he made the whole bed shake.
"I come to watch you die." he said; then he pulled a chair up near
      my bed.
"How long do you think this is going to take?"

To tell you the truth, I was feeling low, and I was even thinkin' it
      was my time to go.
I don't recall having ever been that sick!
But I laughed despite the shape I was in, when he pulled out a
      Sudoku and a ball-point pen.
Shouted "8" and laughed like a lunatic!

It was almost more than I could bear! He looked like a big old kid
      at the county fair.
And I was startin' to feel like I'm the main attraction!
"You ain't going to watch me die!" I said, "Hell! I'm a loooong
      way from dead!"
I sure wasn't gonna give HIM that satisfaction!

I pulled myself around 'till I was sitting up, took a
long drink from
          my sippy cup,
And gave him my very best "go-to-Hades" look.
He dragged the gimme cap off his old bald head,
rubbed his chin,
          and grinned and said
"Stripers are running down on Sharkey's Nook."

Now, I don't know much about psychology, and
medicine is
          science way beyond me
But I started feeling better right then and there!
You know it's been five years since we had a good
run, and I sure
          hated missing all that fun,
I said, "Hand me that crutch, and get out of my
hair!"

He flashed me a gap-toothed grin and said, "I
thought that'd get
          you out of that bed!"
I said, "No! I just gotta go take a pee!"
"Well, you're pissin' your life away" he said,
"Might as well get
          back in that bed,
And will all your fishin' gear to me!"

"I never said I was gonna die! But, I'm sure enough
sick, and that
          ain't no lie!
But I've sort of been feeling a little bit … confined.

A change of pace is what I need, and if them
stripers are startin' to
          feed,
Why, we'd better go hook 'em before they change
their mind!"

He smiled like he won something big. I knew he
couldn't resist
          another dig
When he picked me up next morning out on the
edge of town.
And every mile we drove south, the only thing that
came outta his
          mouth
Was, "Do you think we need to stop, or turn
around?"

I ignored his jabs as he knew I would. I'd a said
something back if
          I thought I could.
I was so glad to cross that Corpus Christi Bridge!
We got to the cabin he said "We're here! I think I'll
have myself a
          beer!"
***** I plumb forgot! ***** I'd left a mouse inside
that fridge!

Oh! He screamed like victim of a stabbin'! Went
ape all over that
          cabin!
He crashed through the door onto the porch out
back.

He went right through the cedar rail, and ended up
flat dab on his
          tail.
He was moaning and groaning about his
sackrowillieack!

Well, I loaded him up in the pickup bed, and gave
him a pillow for
          his old bald head,
He kept askin', "How'd that get inside there?"
I felt real guilty about that rat, but I thought I'd
better not mention
          that.
I just looked up at the sky and said, "Smell that
sweet Gulf air!"

I finally got him home in his own little bed, "I guess
I better go." I
          said.
I was afraid he'd see the guilt written on my face.
When I got to his house the very next day, I didn't
know what I
          was going to say.
But you know, sometimes, the words just seem to
fall in place.

I walked right in like I owned the place, and got
right down there
          in his face.

74

I bumped around and I made the whole bed shake.
"I come to watch you die." I said; then I pulled a
chair up near his
           bed.
"How long do you think this is going to take?"

Stone Face

Why have I a face of stone that never cracks a
smile?
While deep inside, if truth be known,
I'm laughing all the while.

Why doth a solemn continence denote a fate so
poor?
Do not hyenas ravage continents
to a worse fate far more sure?

Does not a ragged smile of sorts cause a baby's face
to drool?
The comedian who treads the boards –
is he not called a fool?

No, thank you very much. I think I shall never grin.
You can think of me as you will.
I think I'll just have a gin.

Love and Other Illusions

Angel's Glow

When I was young, back on the farm, I'd play out in
the yard
On summer nights, catch fireflies, and put them in a
jar.
And Mama would tell me stories about angel lights,
and I'd have
      to let them go.
But I felt safe within my angel's glow.

I'd take one or two back to my room, so Mama
wouldn't know.
And I'd fall asleep within my angel's glow.

Then, I grew up and met my wife. The love of my
life.
On summer nights I was mesmerized by fireflies in
her eyes.
And Mama's stories, about those angel lights, I
believed that they
      were so.
And I'd fall asleep at night within my angel's glow.

We were young, it's true, but we both knew, I'd
never let her go.
And I felt safe within my angel's glow.

Then heaven called my angel home, and left me on
my own.
But summer nights and fireflies, tell me I'm not
alone,
And Mama's stories about those angel lights, I
know now that it's
            so!
And I feel safe within my angel's glow.

I'll catch one or two like I always do, but before I
let them go.
I'll fall asleep tonight within my angel's glow.

Between the Sky and the Deep Blue Sea

Between the sky
And the deep blue sea,
I stood and pledged
My troth to thee.
And though the years have passed,
I can't forget.
I loved you then
And I love you yet.

You ask me if I still love you.
I'll tell you now, and tell you true.
Until all time should reach an end,
And even if you ask me then,
In that last moment, I'll swear I do!

And I know that you will be loving
me
Between the sky and the deep blue
sea.

Forbidden Dreams

Forbidden dreams of unspoken things, of treasures undiscovered.
Such sweet, sweet things the nighttime brings; of pleasures long
      covered.
Loves kept at bay in the light of day, at night come fresh alive.
Secrets bold in the light untold, in the midnight darkness thrive.

If I loved you, would I be untrue if another was well thought of?
If love is wrong when felt so strong then why even call it love?
Love should not a prison be; the soul not be confined.
The heart heeds what the soul needs, and cannot be defined.

Why must love be parceled out, or rationed forth like gold,
Claimed, and staked, and all fenced in, until the blood within runs
      cold?
What, in light of day, is kept away, by guilt and fear and lies,
Late at night when the soul takes flight, the lonely

spirit cries.

Oh! Come back to me on the midnight breeze that
sooths the still-
          shut eye.

The memory slows. The weakness grows.
But the dreams, … They stay alive.

Have You Seen the Mountains?

Have you ever seen the mountains, or the deep blue
skies?
Or the look within your lover's eyes
And wished to never see those things again?
Have you seen the sun, or the moon rise?
Or the salted tears of sweet surprise,
And not have the scene etched in your brain?
Nor have I.

Have you ever heard a baby laugh?
Or the bawling cry of a newborn calf,
And wished to never hear those things again?
Have you heard her say, "I love you!"
Or the sweet reply, "I love you too."
And not have those words engraved in your brain?
Nor have I.

Have you ever smelled the grass new-mown?
Or, biscuits and coffee on a Sunday morn
And wished to never smell such things again?
Have you smelled the ocean in all its breadth?
Or the sweet, sweet smell of a puppy's breath
And not have that scent fixed in your brain?
Nor have I.

Have you ever had lemonade on a hot, hot day?
Or licked an ice cream cone before it melted away
And wished to never have that taste again?
Have you ever kissed her in a summer rain,
And tasted her lips like sweet champagne,
And not have that taste sealed in your brain?

Nor have I.

Have you ever felt like you could fly?
Or been so happy you could almost cry,
And wished to never feel that way again?
Have you touched your lover until she glowed
Or ever been touched like you were gold,
And not have that feeling burned into your brain?
Nor have I.

My Grandmother's Voice

At a party the other night,
On the patio, flooded with soft moonlight,
I heard the sweet,
     unmistakable,
        distinctive sound
Of my grandmother's voice.

It was music to my ears.
My grandmother has been dead for more than
twenty years.

She didn't return to reveal startling revelations.
Just words and phrases and stray pieces of other's
conversations.
She didn't say a lot in
      that voice I had
        almost
forgot.

But it was she. It brought me to tears.

No, I didn't see her. It was just the voice,
But it was so nice to hear her again after all these
years.

I'll Give In

I don't trust myself alone.
I should pay my tab, get up, and just go home.
Because I know where this will end;
When she dances with me slow, I'll give in.

I'll give in to passions call.
I won't think about the ones I hurt at all.
I just can't hide this urge within.
When she looks into my eyes, I'll give in.

I don't want to be this way.
Wish I could just stand up and crawl away.
It's a game nobody wins.
When I hear her breathe my name, I'll give in.

I'll give in and I'll sink low,
And I'll hate myself the farther down I go.
I'll cross a line that just won't bend.
When I feel her lips on mine, I'll give in.

I'll give in to passion's call.
No, I won't think about the ones at home at all.
It's been so long I've held this in.
Even though I know it's wrong, I'll give in.

I'll give in. Yes, I'll give in.
I'll be somewhere lost in time and deep in sin.
I'll give in yes, I'll give in.
With her body touching mine, I'll give in.

Moonlit Arabesque

A blue-jeaned girl and a purloined egg are rustic
barnyard scenes.
Low, she bows, as if to beg her gifts from feathered
queens.
With graceful form; an untrained grace that comes
to pure of heart,
Behind the barn, she takes her place and awaits the
music's start.

A darkened cloud like a curtain parts to reveal a
spotlight moon.
A cricket maestros' music starts as frogs begin to
tune.
A barefoot girl then makes a pass across the loft to
pose,
And holds a perfect arabesque with tangled hair and
dirt streaked toes.

All day long, she has groomed her act preparing for
the show.
A show obscured by a secret pact. Only the hens
will know.
She dreams the dreams of little girls as she does her
ballet mime.
She never dreams that a dream unfurls without
regard for time.

Years have passed since dreams came true.
(Dreams don't always end in doom.)
Now the barefoot girl wears satin shoes beneath an
electric moon.
She dreamt her dream, and took her chance where
people sit in rows.
And she dreams of when she used to dance in the
moonlight with dirt streaked toes.

Winner, bronze award, Greater New Braunfels Arts Council,
April 2000

Obstacle Illusion

I tried leaving you a thousand times,
But you're a hill I just can't seem to climb.
Every time I run into a wall
I sooth my aching heart in alcohol.
And I pretend that you're still with me yet,
So I don't have to work hard to forget.
It don't seem to matter what I do,
I can't get over loving you.

You're an obstacle illusion.
You're a bourbon based solution.
You're not really even here at all.
You're just a figment of the alcohol.
If you don't leave, I can't get over you.
And if you do, I don't know what I'll do.
So if you'll pardon my conclusion,
You're just an obstacle illusion.

Time on My Hands

With time on my hands, I started the day, with nothing to do
but sit there and pray.
What would become of this lonely old man with nothing to
do but look at my hands?
There by my thumb, an elongated scar, one I brought back
from a long-ago war.
A lasting memento from faraway lands for a soldier of
fortune with time on his hands.

Liver spots freckle my leathery old skin. The knuckles are
knobby and ugly as sin.
Age has set in, and it came quite unplanned. Oh the story
that shows the time on my hands.
I quit biting my nails a little while back so they look much
better as a matter of fact.
There's a deep little groove beneath my wedding band,
caused by the time it's been on my hand.

I could count on my fingers the times I've prevailed; I can
point at myself for the times I have failed.
I could snap my fingers in time with a band; I can do
meaningless things with time on my hands.
I could tap my fingers on the arm of the chair. I could
twiddle my thumbs and no one would care.
I could scribble a note in the slow shifting sands. I could
rage at the clock for its fast moving hands.

Doctor says she can come home today, so I guess He does
listen to me when I pray.
I've got some more time with her now, and that's grand!

Like two kids in love, we go off hand-in-hand.
The world is our oyster! We can go anywhere, but the pearls
are so useless with no one to share.
But we've got each other, and our little plans. I'm grateful
for plenty of time on our hands.

Have We Loved it All Away

Have we loved it all away? Is there nothing left
inside?
Is there something I can say to bring the love back
to your eyes?
I thought our love would last forever,
Now you don't have a word to say.
As we sit here in the silence,
Did we love it all away?

I thought if I never cheated, I thought if we never
lied,
We would always have each other; our love would
stand the test of time.
Now you won't let me hold you.
Won't let me kiss those tears away.
In the cold and lonely darkness,
Have we loved it all away?

Now you say that you still love me, And God
knows I still love you.
But you won't even touch me and it breaks my heart
in two.
No one told me to be careful;
To save some for a rainy day.
I took too much and gave too little.
I guess I loved it all away.

Have we loved it all way? Is there nothing left
inside?

Is there something I can say to bring the love back
to your eyes?
I thought our love would last forever,
Now we don't have a word to say.
As we sit here in the darkness,
Did we love it all away?

As we go to sleep this evening
All I can do is pray
That we'll find on a new morning
We haven't loved it all away.

I Do!

There a rumor going round you been running over
town,
Hanging out with all your friends.
No need for you to hide 'cause you're a free woman
now!
Ain't no need for you to pretend.
They ask you if you're missing all my huggin' and
my kissin'.
They asked you if you ever cry.
A friend of mine said you looked her in the eye and
said,
"Never let 'em see you cry!"

Well, maybe you don't cry, but I do.
I ain't afraid to let you know.
Maybe you don't hurt like I do, baby,
Or maybe you don't want me to know.

Maybe you don't lie awake nights,
And maybe your days ain't blue.
Maybe it's true – you don't cry – but I do!

If You Didn't Love Me

If you didn't love me, wouldn't nobody love me.
If you didn't know me then I'd be somebody that
nobody knows.
If you didn't need me, wouldn't nobody need me.
And if you didn't love me baby, wouldn't nobody
love me at all.

You cried on my shoulder. We never felt closer.
If you didn't catch me, no telling how far I would
fall.
If you didn't hold me, wouldn't nobody hold me.
And if you didn't love me, baby, wouldn't nobody
love me at all.

If you didn't miss me, wouldn't nobody miss me.
If you didn't phone me, wouldn't nobody call me at
all.
If you didn't kiss me, wouldn't nobody kiss me.
And if you didn't love me, baby, wouldn't nobody
love me at all.

Just For Me

Early each morning you stand by your window,
And give me a view of the sun shining through
Your hair that you wear just for me.
I sit in my room, and I play my guitar,
Singing a song that I wrote just for you
And you hair, that you wear, just for me.

I can't count the times that I wished you were mine.
I can't count the diamonds that sparkle and shine
In your hair that you wear just for me.

Watching the morning turn into day,
I find I'm unable to turn away
From your smile. Ah, you smile, just for me.
Soon you'll be ready to turn and go in,
And I'll wait for morning to live once again
All the while in your smile just for me.

I can't count the times that I wished you were mine.
I can't count the diamonds that sparkle and shine
In your smile, in your smile, just for me.

Watching the morning turn into day,
I find I'm unable to turn away.
Your love lies in your eyes just for me.
Though you are married, and I know it's a sin
I just can't wait to be with you again.
Your love lies in your eyes just for me.

I can't count the times that I wished you were mine.
I can't count the diamonds that sparkle and shine
In your eyes, in your eyes, just for me.

When She Loves

I'm the one she comes to – when she comes to.
She leans on me when push comes to shove.
I'm the one she wants when she wants too,
And, I'm the one she loves when she loves.

I've always come in second to the bottle.
Jim Beam has always been her first love.
But when she gets way down, and hits the bottom,
Then she comes around and wants my love.

And I'm the one she comes to – when she comes
too.
She leans on me when push comes to shove.
I'm the one she wants when she wants too,
And, I'm the one she loves when she loves.

You know, I'm the one she loves when she loves.

Special Forces

Reconnoiter

The soldier viewed the battlefield
With fear and pain and loathing,
And prayed he would not be
revealed --
A lamb in wolf's clothing.

We broke the sixth and maybe ten,
And abetted number eight.
Man's inhumanity unto man.
Sin and hate and fate

Then, when our tortured sins we tell
At the foot of the throne of God,
Will we be cast into timeless hell
To walk the coals unshod?

Or will we will find a fount of grace

Where mercy is freely given?
Will we find love in the Father's
face,
And at last find peace in heaven?

When, at last, my treasured flag they
crease,
And solemn "TAPS" is played,

                              Will the shame of
heroes ever cease?
                    Will the coward's courage fade?

Special Forces

The patient writhed in pain, and tears, and agony.
Pain, far more than we could feel.
    Tears, far more than we could cry.
        Agony, far more than we could imagine.

Like first responders with all the answers we peeled
back the ugly wound.
With napalm and snake eye bombs, we un-jungled
the disease that brought the
Pain, far more than we would feel;
    Tears, far more than we would cry;
        Agony, far more than we would imagine.

The fetid blood flowed like a crimson tide that
engulfed us all.
We escaped the disease but the sickness endures;
but we had to try
To staunch the blood; we had to try to stop the
Pain, far more than we should feel;
    Tears, far more than we should cry;
        Agony, far more than we should imagine.

The patient died of course, but her daughter lives
on.
And, we brought home the sickness that has been
borne for fifty years.
Crippled bodies, laden hearts, and tortured minds of
those who now endure

The pain, far more than we can feel;
The tears, far more than we can cry;
The agony, far more than we can imagine.

The Helmet at Duc Lap

A helmet lay upon the battlefield;
Lost or abandoned like Archilochus'
shield.
And I, a Saion, a white knight, off to
save someone,
A Paladin, I took the helmet, and left
the gun.

It was perfectly good this enemy's
lid,
And perfectly ironic the message it
hid.
For inscribed within were a palm tree
and a dove.
Ancient symbols of peace and love.

Why would our sworn and deadly
foe
Have such symbols? I would never
know.
And, why should I care for that lost
enemy pot?
Except, as the victor I should exult
not.

And by delighting in things that were

truly delights
I kept the thing with me through long
days and nights.
(My soul, my soul!) Disturbed by
sorrows that could not be consoled
And for forty years harbored a
grudge uncontrolled.

But I finally found comfort from the
message within
And at last returned the helmet to
that lost soldier's kin.
And in the peaceful rhythm that
controls all men's lives
I found another Shield, no worse, but
One far more wise.

Author's note: Duc Lap was a Special Forces camp on a hill in Viet Nam three miles out of Cambodia that guarded two heavily traveled trails into South Viet Nam. Because this vantage point hampered movement into the South, the North Vietnamese Army (NVA) needed to control that place. Largely defended by Montagnards and other mountain tribes, they were assisted by advisors who called the site Camp A-239. The attack

*began in late August 1968, and the
defenders were push to the southern
ridge, until special strike forces
could come to the rescue and
enabled them to retake the valuable
position. Over 800 enemy were
killed in the battle. Assigned to a
special team of "advisors", Sergeant
John Wast, the only American in
the group of mostly Australian
forces, picked up a helmet of a dead
NVA soldier as a souvenir. Inside
were inscribed the soldier's name,
and symbols of a dove and a palm
tree. In 2012 Sergeant Wast, and
the DOVE Fund began looking for
the soldier's family, and through
the efforts of that healing
organization, the helmet was
eventually returned to the lost
soldier's family in a village just
outside Hanoi. This poem is a
fictional account of that actual
event, borrowing heavily on
passages from Archilochus who
described an abandoned shield on a
Greek battlefield. A Saion, or
Paladin, defeated their enemies and
used white magic to heal, similar to
our modern warrior battlefield
medics who use medicine to heal the
wounded. Sgt. Wast was Platoon
Leader and was acting as medic*

__with 212 MSF Company at the time.__
__Thank you, John, for helping me__
__tell this story.__

*First appeared, Art of Peace Poetry Anthology, __Intertwined__,
2015*

Once Again He Arises

Once again, he arises
Wafting above the waves of pain.
Like a chrysalis clinging to a climbing stalk,
He emerges; wings outspread to face the day,
Ready once more, to fly again.

Once again, he rises.
The gain outweighs the pain.
Cleaving upward through the clinging, cloying, fog
And, in the face of grace, receives the lifting, loving
hand,
Ready once more, to live again.

Terminus

When at last refrains the Herald's horn
Across the boundless plain.
Could moments lost -
Would life reborn
At any cost -
Glorify the gain?

Do not expect this wretched form
To rise up to fight again.

Waiting for Nurse Godot

The orderly said he would send her by with just a little
something for the
       pain.
How long ago, I do not know. He turned off the light
when he left again,
And I can't see the clock. It was four in the morning
when he left, and if
       I didn't hurt
I could go back to sleep. Therapy comes with the
morning sun, and I
       must be ready to work.

Maybe he forgot to tell her. It could be he got busy and
forgot.
Or, perhaps someone else needs her far more than I do at
4 o'clock.
I'm sure she will be by soon with the merciful dose that
kills the pain
That takes me off to dreamland again.

Should I push the button by my bed – in case he did
forget? Should I be
       bolder?
I'm sure she would have been here by now – if he had
told her.
She is probably on her way right now, bringing the pain
relief prn.
Any moment now that big wooden door will swing open,
and she'll walk
       in.

Did he write the room number down right?
What if he wrote 224 instead of 242? They are a lot
alike.

If she went to 224 and found that man did not complain,
She may think I no longer need help with the pain.

If he remembered to tell her; if he didn't get side tracked
somehow.
If I can find that button here in the dark, I'll ring again
right now.
Surely, it wasn't on purpose – I know he wouldn't be
unkind.
Something important must have happened to cause it to
slip his mind.

There! Now, Nurse Godot will come for sure. It won't
be long and she'll
          be here.
There is no mistaking the button – it must flash a light
somewhere.
When she sees the light, she will surely come – she can't
help but see.
No worry about the room number, the light will guide
her right to me.

That is – if the light is working. Is it working? Please tell
me that it
          works.
Is there something wrong with the button? God, how
awful my leg hurts.
How would they know I needed something for the pain
now?
How would they know I was lying here in the dark with
sweat on my

brow?

I wonder if Nurse Godot is really there? Maybe she left
for the night.
Maybe they are out of medicine, and they have nothing
left on-site.
Does a hospital run out of medicine? They must from
time to time,
Especially if someone uses far more than they expected,
especially at
        nighttime.

It must have been at least an hour! I lie here helpless
with no power.
I can't see the clock in the dark, but I'm sure it must be
at least an hour.
The pain is getting worse, and it is hard to move my leg.
I am glad I am not dying. I could die here in the dark and
no one here to
        beg.

How does it get darker than dark? Things seem to be
growing dimmer.
You'd think the sky would be getting light outside, but
the window
        shows no glimmer.
It is quiet; no noise that I can hear. No one is coming
down the hall,
And the dark on dark continues to grow into oblivion.
Deep … dark …
        void. That is all.

*Nurses log: Rm 242, Pt requested prn pain relief 0403.
Arrived 0405, patient sleeping peacefully. Deferred*

administration of prn until patient wakes. Lt. Godot, R.N.

The Host

The pounding sound of the rotor blade
Whirls deep within my chest.
I cling, now safely, unafraid,
Rising high above the test.
What once seemed huge and insurmountable,
Now shrinks away below,
To return at night with dreams of uncountable
Echoes within my soul.
The pinging thumps of small arms fire, like useless
ghosts,
Fall harmless from the fray,
And I, within the shelter of the host –
I'm lifted safe away.

■■

The awesome power of the world displayed
Churns deep within my breast.
I walk upright and unafraid,
For I know now I am blessed.
What once seemed huge and overwhelming,
Now shrinks away below,
And in the night, now strangely calming,
All is well within my soul.
The stinging bumps of life, like toothless ghosts,
Fall harmless from the fray,
And I, within the shelter of the Host –
I'm lifted safe away.

The True-badour

A Nation Burning

We set our cities burning, as toward the past we
keep on turning
With a thousand hearts a churning, will we learn
from what came before?
Or, will our future be uncast due to hardships of the
past,
Or will we finally see at last that the future holds
much more?
Our future as a nation holds much more.

Will the fire avenge the pain? Will the cost out-strip
the gain?
Will our liberties remain, as we hurl our laws onto
the floor?
Are we slave to senseless rage? Can we not read the
written page?
Does the violence here upstage the real questions
we implore?
Does our future as a nation hold much more?

Is it all reduced to black and white? Is that the
reason we fight?
Can anger ever fully right all the suffering that
came before?
On a horse of fear, the anger rides, and wretched
fear affects both sides.

Is it more important to take sides, or to strive for
something more?
Does our future as a nation hold much more?

Can't we agree to disagree, and yet retain our
liberty?
Are we so inept we cannot see the ruin at our door?
When, in righteous indignation, race is chosen over
nation,
It always ends in conflagration – only this, and
nothing more.
Does our future as a nation hold much more?

The Edge of Town

Here, on the edge of town, I've found that towns
don't have edges anymore.
Once, a thousand yards from the city limit sign was
out in the country,
The domain of egg farmers and produce sellers by
the side of the road.
When I was a boy, I sold watermelons on Highway
6 outside Hempstead;
sweet, firm, and ripe, and so full of juice it would
burst open with one slice of the knife.

Now towns have fringes; fingers of population
stringing along every road out of town;
The domain of strip malls and convenience store
gas stations.
Pay at the pump. No need for cash.
Neon signs illuminate the drive-through fast-food
chains.
No need to get out of the car.
No chance to meet anyone; see anyone; know
anyone.
No watermelon and the eggs aren't fresh.

Next Plane South

Baby, I'm in love with you, but there's just a little
something that I gotta do. I'm leaving in the morning,
headin' on the next plane south.
Baby, you been good to me, but there's a little piece of
paradise where I've gotta be. I'm leaving in the morning,
headin' on the next plane south.
I'm leaving in the morning, headin' on the next plane
south.

The next plane south, where the palm trees grow. South
of Miami there ain't no snow.
So, I'm leaving in the morning, headin' on the next
plane south.
I'll be leaving in the morning, headin' on the next plane
south.

Baby, there ain't no hurricane keep this country boy
from going home again. You know, I'm leaving in the
morning, headin' on the next plane south.
Baby, I sure hate to leave, but this big city air is just too
hard to breathe
So, I'll be leaving in the morning, headin' on the next
plane south.
I am leaving in the morning, headin' on the next plane
south.

The next plane south where the seawater's green.
Prettiest place I've ever seen. And I'm leaving in the
morning, headin' on the next plane south.
Oh, I'm leaving in the morning, headin' on the next
plane south.

Baby, you're a big city girl, but there's a whole lot more

to this big old world. Why don't you meet me in the morning? We'll leave on the next plane south.
Baby, come along with me, we'll swim in the sunset off Little Torche Key. We can in the morning, headin' on the next plane south.
Yeah, Let's leave in the morning, headin' on the next plane south.

The next plane south where the sea breeze blows. We'll be making love in the coconut groves, Meet me in the morning, and we'll leave on the next plane south.
Yes, I'm leaving in the morning, headin' on the next plane south.

Southern Secrets

In the south, we have our secrets – and we know
how to keep them too.
If we wanted you to know what we were thinking,
we'd be talking.
And, we don't go around digging up old bones.
We leave them dead and buried where they belong.
If we dug them up, we might find whatever put
them in the ground
Might still be around.

Out on the creeks and bayous, the silver
moonbeams
Drip like earrings beneath the Spanish moss,
Where a week on either side of full,
The un-jeweled hag's hair hangs
In the shadows of the moon.

Where invisible things make concentric rings on the
dark shadowed water,
Which spread away to distant shores
To lip the far-away sands
And quietly die.
Like our secrets.

Too Far Gone to Care

On rainy nights, the car lights reflect off cold wet
streets.
Drinking wine helps pass the time, and makes my
day complete.
I pull the plug, take another slug, and my worries
disappear.
I'm a thousand drinks away, and too far gone to
care.
A thousand drinks away and too far gone to care.

Keeping up with a girl like her can keep you on the
run.
She said she ain't done nothing wrong, she just likes
to have some fun.
Well, it's time I learned, so now it's my turn, and
it's the best I've had in years.
I'm a thousand tears away, and too far gone to care.
I'm a thousand tears away, and too far gone to care.

How times I bought her lines. I guess I heard them
all.
And lately, I've been wondering if she can tell the
truth at all.
She called at eight, said she's working late, but I
know that she's not there.
I'm a thousand lies away, and too far gone to care.
I'm a thousand lies away, and too far gone to care.

How many times did I tell her that one day I would
leave?
She just looked right through me. She did not
believe.
So, today's the day I fly away so high up in the air.
I'm a thousand miles away, and too far gone to care.
I'm a thousand miles away from her, and too far
gone to care.

Savannah Beach on Tybee Isle

Savannah Beach on Tybee Isle,
Where old meets new to reconcile.
From who knows where the shells float in?
The tide rolls out and comes back again.
As will I, one day, just like the geese,
When I seek solitude and peace.
With the top rolled down, and hair a fright,
Like thunder, I'll roll in one summer night.
I'll throw my cares to the ocean wind
And make sweet memories once again.

Heroes and Outlaws

Alamo Blue

There is a certain azure color that spreads before the
dawn
In the eastern morning sky above the town of San
Antone.
At the end of winter's wanting and before the spring
winds blow
You can hear the ghostlike fiddles playing from the
Alamo.

A campfire snaps and flickers, casting shadows on
the wall
To reveal the dancing figures of the men who hailed
the call.
As they wait there in the darkness for the end they
know will come
They laugh, and drink, and dance in the time before
the sun.

No regrets, no fear, no anguish as they wait the
coming morn,
And they vow to keep on fighting until the angel
blows his horn.
In the black and frosty hours, they can hear the
battle sound
As the caissons and the cannon are positioned all
around.

The devil rides a cold white stallion, before three
thousand men
To face the limestone walls that hold one eighty
there within.
Then the notes of El Deguello drown out the
fiddle's song,
As the men lay aside their music to prepare to face
the throng.

They know what waits the morning, just as sure as
sun comes up.
They know without the telling that they've drunk
their final cup.
Bayonets and bullets await them one and all,
But, they'll take a few more with them before their
final fall.

The thunder of the cannon and a fiery blast of light
Opens up the battle in the pale and fading night.
Fingers tightly clutching heavy rifles by their side
They stand and hold their places and face the
coming tide.

They say their final prayers. They know their lives
are through.
They turn and face toward heaven, and that certain
azure blue.
In a massive funeral pyre on that bitter Sunday
morn,
When the smoke curled up to heaven, an angel blew
his horn.

There are those before and after, who have faced
their destiny
To give their final service to the cause of liberty.
But none more sure or brave, as they watched their
life blood flow,
And none held more in reverence than the men of
Alamo.

There is a certain azure color that spreads before the
dawn
In the eastern morning sky above the town of San
Antone.
At the end of winter's wanting and before the spring
winds blow
You can hear the ghostlike fiddles playing from the
Alamo.

In the Antitheses of the Dawn

When you have given all that you can give,

And you have done your very best;
When you have sanctified the life you live;
Then you may lie at last, and rest.

The Legend of Elfego Baca

North of Silver City flows the forked Gila,
Southwest across the desert toward Yuma
Into the mighty Colorado.
Gun smoke blue water slides past smoothed rock –
slides so fast,
Like cold blue steel on worn, tanned leather – slides
so fast.
Hammer cocked – trigger fingered before it leaves
the nest.

Beneath the towering, rocky, heights of San
Francisco
Lies a lost and forgotten wilderness of canyon and
arroyo.
There, where deer fade into the leafy forest like
memories
Lies the sleepy village they called Frisco.
Faded now from long ago – as memories fade and
go –
Like the name of Elfego.

Even the name of the town has come and gone.
It has not been called Frisco for, oh so long.
It never was the name of the town, you see, at all.
Once was Middle Plaza of San Francisco.
Not the famous place you may have heard in song.
A place of destiny for Elfego.

Cowboys rode west to work the dusty cattle trails.
Surely even you have heard the legends and tails

Of bloody wars of water, and range, and fence.
Of outcast and outlaw, desperado and caballero;
Of Garret and the Kid, and all they did. But what of
the tales
Of the man they called Elfego?

The riders hated Mexicans, and delighted in their
fear.
They even changed one paisano from a bull into a
steer.
Day and night, they lived to drink and loved to
fight.
Calls for help went afar, but the only one to wear
the star and go;
The only one who dared come near
Was the fabled Elfego

The outlaws could hear his spurs a block away,
But Charlie McCarty was too drunk that day,
And too blind to see the danger come.
And too dumb to even know,
And, was not listening anyway.
To the spurs of Elfego.

With a self-made badge, this self-appointed law
Arrested Charlie, shooting up the mall.
And, eighty cowboys came to set him free.
"Why don't we hang that little Mexican so-and-so?"
"Why don't you try?" he said with lightning draw.
Just try to hang Elfego.

Elfego took refuge in an adobe jacal
As four thousand rounds went through his wall.

Eighty to one were the odds that day.
But like the fables of el gato,
If he had nine lives that day he used them all.
Not a single bullet hit Elfego.

His roof they burned, his walls they clove.
From the rabbled heap thick smoke arose.
And, in the morning light of the red streaked sky
He was flipping tortillas over red hot coals,
On a bullet riddled, cast-iron stove!
Breakfast for Elfego.

He survived the most lopsided war in history.
How he lived through that is still a mystery.
They never killed him – even once!
They tried four thousand times though.
In the end the final victory
Was won by Elfego.

Elfego walked away, and lived to fight another day.
He once shot a man three hundred yards away.
When asked to tell the outlaw's name,
Elfego said he didn't know.
By the time Elfego reached his side, the outlaw
couldn't say.
He never told Elfego.

In the end, he took to fame, whisky, and song
And all the women who were drawn

The legend and the name of a hero.
The smoky memories slide quickly past – fade so
fast,
Like cold blue steel on worn, tanned leather – slides
so fast.
Hammer cocked – trigger fingered before it leaves
the nest.
So, the legend of Elfego.

My Dad the Dinosaur

He was a man's man first and always. He had tough old
dinosaur hide.
I don't think he ever cried, not even when his youngest
son died.
That did not mean he did not feel or hurt.
He just went back to work.
He was all hard bone and knuckles.
No one ever called HIM a jerk.

He was no bully, and never made threats. He lived his
life, and kept his Regrets close to his chest. He kept
moving ahead, he never backed up.
He would give you
the shirt off his back,
but he wouldn't be pushed,
not even an inch.

His word was his bond. If he said it, he made it happen.
If he couldn't he wouldn't even say it. But if he did,
You could take it to the bank.
He did not expect or want you to thank
or even pay him anything. His biggest fault was
he expected you to be the same.

He wasn't tall, but it shouldn't surprise, men like him
aren't judged by their size. He never met a stranger, He
never pointed a finger,
and he never judged without cause –
not even, sometimes, if there was one.
If you needed help there was never a pause.
He pitched right in and got it done.

He was a throw back from way back. When he was old,
he tried hard to hold on to the only way of life he ever
knew.
One that was true; red, white and blue. When he died of
emphysema, he died hard.
I counted a line of cars two miles long
on the way to the graveyard
to bury a dinosaur.

I Want to Be Like Tonto

Tonto was always ready to help. He was never far away.

Tonto never said no to a friend or good person in need.

Tonto did whatever was needed without worrying about consequences.

Tonto never asked "why?" first.

Lone Ranger never had to say, "Thank you."
Tonto knew.

Lone Ranger never had to say, "I'm sorry." Tonto knew that too.

Tonto never asked for more than he needed.

Tonto never asked for, or expected anything in return.

Tonto kept the Lone Ranger's secrets.

Tonto never put himself first.

I want to be like Tonto.

On the Death of Friends

I guess I'm at that time of my life
where I lose a friend almost every week.
People we thought would always be around –
suddenly gone, and we are left alone
to carry on without them in our lives.
Why didn't I call yesterday?
Why didn't I drop around for that chat?
Why didn't I reach out and let them know I care?
The game of life got in the way,
and death ended the game – like it will for us all.
But that doesn't make it any easier.

Sometimes death comes as a welcome relief –
A respite from a life of pain and suffering.
Sometimes death sneaks up on us
Like a lightning bolt from the blue.
Here one minute – gone the next.
Off on a glorious ride to eternity – good or bad.
Either way, it's always sad – for those left behind.
We always say they are in a better place now.
But that doesn't make it any easier.

So on and on we go – until it is our time to go.
We promise to do better – to pay more attention
To the people important in our lives.
If I knew then what I know now … that all my
friends
Would fall, like leaves from a tree,
I would have made a lot more friends – planted

more trees.
I would have been much kinder – far less critical.
I would have been the kind of friend
I would hope to have – and should be now.
They would have left knowing they were loved.

But that doesn't make it any easier.

Let Me Count the Ways

South of West, Toward Paradise

When the sun sets a little south of west,
leaves the sky a glowing shade of translucent blue
where blackened, silhouetted hills form a vee
through the pass
leading the way along the path I want to take.
Oh! So nice. .. Toward paradise.

While high above, the evening star glimmers and
gleams like a diamond,
not unlike the crystalline jewel on your creamy
breast
above the satin, silky vee of your sequined gown
leading the way along the path I want to take.
Oh! So nice… Toward paradise.

Forever Loves

Some loves come for such a short affair.
Some loves come and go like air.
Some loves come in answer to a prayer.
But forever loves are always there.

Forever loves are the air we breathe,
The songs we sing, the truths we believe,
The realization of the future we perceive;
The home our dreams conceive.

Nothing or anyone can ever rise above
Our hearts greatest joy: our forever loves.

Alarms

The moonlight through the Live Oak trees
Sets off the ever watchful eye.
The safety light snaps on in the night
To warn of would-be harm.

Nothing moving in the dark on patio or yard.
Fears are safely put away.
A false alarm that did no harm.
I'll return to bed and sleep 'til break of day.

But, the moonlight through the Live Oak trees
Sets off the beauty of your charms.

Another light comes on and I recall
The feeling your love warms.

Nothing I have in my whole life, nor anything I may
be
Can amplify the life your love adorns.
Fears are safely put away, and soundly sleep 'til
break of day
In the warmth of your loving arms.

Ernie Lee is a Texas award winning poet known as the Bard of the Blanco. He lives and writes in the scenic Texas hill country. Many of his poems describe hill country scenes. His poems also tell the stories of his travels around the world. As a twenty-two year veteran of the U.S. Air Force, Ernie has written several pieces from the Viet Nam era. Ernie is a cancer survivor who also writes about facing destiny. His versatile style of poetry ranges from serious and philosophical to rollicking good humor. Ernie's poetry reflects his love of life, interesting places he has been, and people of all backgrounds.

He resides in Canyon Lake, Texas, with his wife, Donna. He is semi-retired and enjoys presenting at schools, poetry festivals, and various events. Ernie began at an early age as a song writer, with some success. His songs are registered with BMI®. He is the producer of the "*Indie Country Road Show*" which can be downloaded from *I-Tunes*. His music can be heard on a website www.reverbnation.com and on MTV as a CMT Artist. In addition, he has written technical and academic text books for the University of Texas (Austin) and UT San Antonio. He has published a dozen professional training workbooks and training materials for professional public procurement officers.

Ernie writes creative short fiction, creative non-fiction, and a lot of poetry. He won two awards from the New Braunfels Arts Council for poetry in 2000 and 2014. He is the 2014 holder of *Lynne Eliot Award for Poetry*. His work has appeared in print many times.

He is a member of the Academy of American Poets, Austin Poets International, Hill Country Poets, Poetry Society of Texas, and the San Antonio Poets Association, and several others. Ernie currently writes a continuing column for the ***Hill Country Sun*** called *The Bard of the Blanco* and a quarterly newsletter entitled **The True-badour**. Through the Writing+Is+Giving program, Ernie selects a worth-while cause for each of his published books, and gives over 2,000 copies free through his website www.ernieleepoetry.com. The goal for 2016, is to give 2,016 copies of the novel *Aquasaurus* to Cancer Fighters because they know hope. This book, **Bard of the Blanco**, will be given to Teachers because they know how to share.

www.ingramcontent.com/pod-product-compliance
Lightning Source LLC
Chambersburg PA
CBHW050148110726
47898CB00008B/2716